Shipwreck on ShadowWorld

David R. Beshears

Greybeard Publishing
Washington State

Greybeard Publishing
P.O. Box 480
McCleary, WA 98557-0480

ISBN 0-9773646-7-4

Shipwreck on ShadowWorld

Chapter One

The ground beneath Jim was hard as stone and there was a small rock digging into his back. The dull red sky of the alien world hung heavy above him. The air felt thick in his lungs.

He rolled to one side and sat up slowly, an inch at a time. The pain in his head pounded at his skull, and the throbbing caused his vision to go fuzzy. It took a few moments to clear. When it did, he looked around him. The small landing craft was a few hundred yards away, fuselage twisted and broken, other unidentifiable debris scattered about the landscape, some of it still burning. He saw no one moving. It took a few moments more for him to realize that he also saw that there was no one who was *not* moving.

From where he was, he could see no bodies.

There had been two other passengers, a man and a woman. They had escaped into the shuttle with him.

Had they been rescued? Had they just left him behind?

Jim guessed that he had been unconscious for a long time; hours at least, maybe longer. He had been thrown a considerable distance from the ship. Maybe they hadn't seen him; but why hadn't they looked for him?

I'm alone...

Jim was thirteen years old. He was slim, strong and healthy. He had been traveling alone, having left Earth three weeks earlier, and was scheduled to arrive at Port Kimara in two weeks. His family would be waiting for him; but he would not be coming home. Not now.

He managed to stand, though his legs were shaky. The ground beneath his feet was bare and hot and dry. The heat of the two suns beat down in waves and made it hard to breath.

Turning about in a slow circle, he could see the rolling terrain spread out and away from him in all directions. He could see for miles... but there was nothing, absolutely nothing, to see.

I'm out in the middle of nowhere... on an alien world.

Jim turned to face the wreckage, took a step and started towards it. Small whorls of smoke rolled across the crash site as the slight breeze pushed the hot alien air over the smoldering ground.

The passenger compartment was split in two and one side of the forward section, the section that Jim had been sitting in, was torn away. He climbed in and looked around, not sure what he was looking for. Water, certainly. He would also be needing food and clothing.

He found nothing in the forward section. The rear section was in even worse condition, but he managed to come out with two water bottles. He stuffed them into his jacket pockets.

What was left of the pilot's cabin was thirty yards from the two sections of the passenger compartment. Jim had to step around torn and twisted metal, broken seats, and viewing ports from the fuselage to reach it. Coming up along the left side, he could see that the forward section of the shuttle hadn't fared any better than the rest of the craft.

Its occupants had fared worse.

Jim looked only very briefly at the two men still strapped in their seats before turning away and walking quickly back to the passenger section of the wreckage.

So there had been at least two casualties.

The pilot and copilot had not survived the crash.

When he returned to the passenger compartments, Jim straightened one of the seats that had been thrown from the cabin and sat down. He brought out one of the water bottles and took a deep drink.

Realization about what had happened began to sink in.

They had crashed. People had died. He still had no idea where the other two had gone.

Had the pirates followed the shuttle down?

Jim doubted that. It was more likely they would have stayed with the cruise ship.

Pirates...

The pirates had attacked the space liner several days before, coming at them in three smaller ships. With no weapons, the cruise ship had no chance.

Only one small landing craft, this shuttle, had managed to slip away. There had been two people in the forward passenger section with Jim; a man and a woman. Jim hadn't known them, but he had seen them around on the liner a few times during the voyage.

They had been lucky to find this planet, but then their luck had run out. Something had gone wrong, and now the small craft was strewn all around him in hundreds of shredded pieces.

Jim laid his head back against the seat and let out a tired sigh.

I can't stay here, he thought.

No one knew that he was there. No one knew where the shuttle had gone down, or even that it had crashed. In all likelihood, no one knew they had come to this planet.

If there had been any survivors, they had left. They wouldn't have left him behind if they had known that he had been there.

Since no one knew that he was there, no one was going to come looking for him. With no food and very little water, he wouldn't last long.

He downed the last of the water from the first bottle and tossed the empty container aside.

He laid his head back and closed his eyes.

The world around him was so quiet. The only sound was the occasional whispering brush of wind across the dry terrain, the empty rustling of torn metal shifting in the breeze.

I have to find help.

He opened his eyes and sat up.

Where do I go?

There was a slight rise to his left, two small to be called a hill. He stood and walked over to it, stood atop and looked around him in all directions.

There... far to the west, set against the horizon, was a small silhouette of something unmoving. It took a moment for the image to come into focus in heavy, hot, shimmering atmosphere.

It was a small peak, just barely visible.

There was nothing else, absolutely nothing else in any direction.

He took one last look back at the wrecked shuttle, then turned uncertainly toward the shadowy silhouette on the horizon. A hundred steps out, he had a strong urge to turn and look back at the crash site. He fought it at first, but finally, after taking another dozen steps, he stopped and turned around.

The broken shuttle was already lost from view. They had crashed in a low-lying shallow hollow.

Jim turned and started walking again.

The ground was hard beneath his feet, the vegetation sparse. Clumps of dry grass and short, spindly brush struggled to survive in the harsh soil beneath two unforgiving suns.

The smudge of shadow that was the peak on the horizon faded into and out of view. With no other landmarks, Jim used the larger sun as a guide, following it as it dropped slowly toward the horizon near the silhouette. Not until it had set, several hours later, did he take a break. There was nothing to sit on, so he dropped down to the ground. It was warm beneath him, but with the setting of the first sun, the air was already beginning to cool.

He took out the second bottle and took a small drink, carefully put the cap back on and put the bottle back in his pocket. He had no idea how long his meager water supply would have to last.

The dull red color of the sky paled. He could feel a slight breeze brush across his face, but there was no sound. The world was absolutely quiet. In spite of the breeze, there was no movement. The grass was still. There were no birds in the sky. There were no insects or small animals scurrying across the ground.

There was nothing.

The smaller sun moved quickly towards the horizon. Reluctantly, he rolled over onto his side and climbed to his feet. He realized then just how tired he was. He considered sitting back down again, but the thought was as unappealing as plodding onward.

He followed the second sun until, not more than an hour later, it too set below the horizon. The color of the sky shifted from its pale red to a dark violet, grew steadily darker until, within minutes, the sky was an empty black canvas.

Jim walked several more minutes before stopping, afraid that if he continued without a landmark of some kind that he would end up walking in circles. Besides, he was too tired to go any further.

He eased himself down to the ground. A few hours rest would do him good. He sat, his weight on one arm, and stared up at the black night sky.

Stars began to appear, more with each passing minute; strange, alien patterns. Before long, the black tapestry above him was filled with thousands upon thousands of stars. The surface of the planet glowed eerily in alien starlight.

The slight, cool breeze grew a little colder, and began to blow just a little harder. The exposed, bare skin of Jim's face began to tingle chillingly. Looking around him, he thought he could see a depression in the ground twenty paces away. He went over to it, stood before it.

It wasn't much of a hole, but it was a bit lower than the surrounding terrain and was protected from the wind on one side by a little rise, several feet high, that formed a tiny hill.

He slid down into the hollow and curled up, covered his face against the increasing cold. Despite his exhaustion, sleep was a long time in coming.

§

There was a strange glow coming from somewhere...

Somewhere...

Daylight. A curious, red daylight...

The glow was the new day shining through his closed eyelids. He felt the warmth of one of the suns washing its warm rays over his face.

Somehow, perhaps subconsciously, he managed to bring his face up to the sunshine. It felt good. He brought his arm up and shaded his still-closed eyes with a cold, icy hand. Slowly then, he opened his eyes.

All was in a bright glare and it took time for his eyes to adjust.

After a few moments more, he sat up straight and began massaging his arms and legs. Looking around, he saw the shadow on the horizon far to the west.

It was still a long ways off, but it was nearer.

He stood up. It hurt. The muscles in his legs were cold, near frozen. He had barely survived the night. He knew that. He knew that he wouldn't be able to survive another, particularly if he was weak from lack of food.

Best to start now and keep moving, he thought. He moistened his cracked lips and started walking. He realized immediately that the cool air was gone, replaced by warm air that was already growing hot. The red, cloudless sky hung heavy over him. His lungs, which had struggled against the cold air of the previous night, now fought against the hot, thick day of this harsh planet.

It was as though there wasn't any oxygen in the air.

He brought out the water bottle as he trudged forward, lifted it to his mouth, let the last of it trickle onto his tongue and soothe the back of his throat.

That's it, then...

He had to find water; he had to find food.

The hours passed and his pace slowed. The morning crept into afternoon. Beyond the peak, the larger sun was very large indeed, painted against the distant sky, still several hours from slipping below the horizon.

The base of the peak was cluttered with hundreds of rocks of all sizes. It towered hundreds of feet over Jim, rising up out of the flat plain, blotting out both suns, the first of which was setting, the smaller following several hours behind the first.

He had to find water soon, and he had to find shelter before nightfall. Backing away from the peak thirty or forty steps, he began walking the perimeter, looking into crevices and shadows for signs of a cave or plant life. Vegetation would mean moisture.

As he came around to the far side of the peak, he saw that the larger of the suns had set. It was still warm on this side, but the air was already growing cooler. He looked at the position of the smaller sun. It would be down in another hour.

The angle of the small sun's rays created strange shadows on the wall of the peak. Jim had to step nearer again and again to make sure that he wasn't missing something.

Then... *was that a sound?*

He stepped close, rested a hand on the rock face. He felt a dull rumbling coming from somewhere deep within the mountain.

There was definitely something in there.

What is that?

Finally, just as the second sun began to disappear below the distant horizon, Jim found the mouth of a cave.

The entrance was ten feet above ground level, but easy to reach. Standing in front of it, the roof of the entrance was just above his head. There was a cool breeze emanating from within, and he could feel moisture in the air.

It was pitch black inside. Going in, Jim had to hold his hands out in front of him so that he wouldn't walk headlong into a wall. Almost immediately, he noticed that the tunnel sloped downward. It gave him the odd sensation that he was being swallowed up by some gigantic alien monster. Only hunger and thirst kept him going. He went slowly, inching his way ahead.

The seconds, and then the minutes, ticked away. Time began weighing heavily on him, down in the darkness, deep within the hollows of this alien place; the tons of stone above him, the pressure of eternity pressing down on him. The fear of spending forever there in that black gut of the peak...

But the air was still fresh. And it continued to grow cooler and smelled of moisture, as after a morning rain. He could feel a dampness, like a mist, against his face. It soothed his dried, cracked lips.

He reached another winding, downward curve in the tunnel, and following it, he began to hear a sound. It was a rumbling, the same rumbling that he had felt beneath his feet since first entering this maze of tunnels; the same rumbling that he had felt when he had pressed his hand against the cliff wall outside.

The further he traveled, still blind in the darkness, the louder the sound became. At first, he dared not hope, but with each passing minute, with each bend in the tunnel, he became more anxious and grew more excited.

Jim stepped into a high-ceilinged cavern. Bands of rock along the walls and ceiling shimmered in their own light. He had heard of phosphorus, a mineral giving off its own peculiar illumination, and guessed that this was something similar, some alien version.

Coursing through the middle of the cavern, an underground river shimmered in the strange darkness, white foam glowing as the water rushed along its underground path.

Jim rushed to the river and stopped short. The surface was a good six feet below the edge of the bank, and it was a sheer drop. Looking up and downriver, he could see no spot where the bank was low enough to make for easy access to the water, but despite the light from the glowing bands of rock in the walls, the cavern was still too dark to see very far.

Turning right, Jim followed the river's edge until it disappeared beneath the wall of the cavern. Finding no access to the water in that direction, he hurried back to the left. He finally found, not far from the opposite wall, a spot where the bank sloped down all the way to the water's edge.

Kneeling, he took a cautious sip. The water was cool and delicious. He took a deeper drink, and then another.

Already feeling a little better, he dipped his head into the water, came up sputtering and smiling. He sat down then and took off his jacket and shirt. He cleaned himself up as best he could, lastly dipping his head into the water again and rinsing his hair.

Refreshed, if still hungry, he climbed up and away from the river, carrying his jacket and shirt. Yes, he needed food, but he needed to rest. He walked over to one wall and dropped his jacket onto the floor, pulled on his wet shirt. He sat then, leaning his back against the wall. He surveyed the cavern, what he could see of it, as he absently rolled his jacket into a makeshift pillow.

Chapter Two

Jim sat bolt upright.

He had been startled by something... awakened by something...

He didn't know what.

He looked carefully around him. The strangely glowing bands of rock within the walls and ceiling continued to illuminate the large chasm. Everything looked as it had when he had fallen asleep. To his left, the river ran from an opening in the wall behind him and disappeared into the darkness at the far end of the cavern. The sound of the river was the only sound.

From where he sat, Jim could see two tunnels, both to his right. The tunnel that he had entered by was further away, hidden in the darkness.

Click, click, click...

Jim stiffened, slid backward and pressed his back against the wall.

The sound had come from one of the tunnels.

Click, click, click...

The sound was louder. Someone, or some *thing*, was coming closer.

Click, click, click...

Jim slid further from the two tunnel entrances and stood, keeping his back against the wall. He couldn't tell from which tunnel the sound came.

Click, click, click...

But it was coming nearer.

He looked quickly around him. His options were limited: He could rush into the darkness, or in the direction of the tunnel that he had come through, or he could jump into the river and take his chances on where it would take him.

Or lastly, he could wait for whatever was in the tunnel to come into the cavern.

He moved quickly away from the wall, toward the middle of the cavern. He turned and faced the two tunnels, the entrances almost side by side, like black, empty eye sockets.

Click, click, click...

Jim took several more steps back, moving further back into the center of the cavern.

The walls deep within one of the tunnels began to glow with artificial light.

Whatever it was, it was bringing its own light with it.

Click, click, click...

A shadow formed within the glow. As it drew nearer the mouth of the tunnel, it started to take shape. The silhouette looked... human-like.

It appeared in the tunnel entrance, took a step into the cavern.

The alien was a small, graying gnome-like creature. Standing a head shorter than Jim, it was dressed in brown robe and cloak, held a lamp in one hand and a wooden staff in the other.

The glowing sphere of yellow light formed by the lamp reached out as far as Jim. The creature stared at him. After several seconds, it tapped its staff on floor of the cavern: *click, click, click.* It waited for some reaction from Jim.

Jim watched all of this uneasily. He had no idea what to make of it.

Click, click, click...

The little man watched and waited.

"Hello," Jim finally stammered.

The little man studied Jim carefully. He took a short step and stopped. "You speak Earth," he said at last. "You are human." These were statements, not questions.

"That's right."

"I am Nebo."

Jim wasn't sure if Nebo was the alien's name or the name of his race.

"My name. I am Nebo."

"I'm Jim."

"What are you doing here? Jim."

"We were attacked." Jim pointed up, as if this would explain that he meant they had been in space. "Pirates. We escaped. We crashed."

"We?" Nebo asked. He looked quickly about the cavern, but could see only Jim.

"I'm alone now. I... I don't know what happened to the others."

"Ah," Nebo nodded thoughtfully.

"I was looking for food and water."

Nebo considered this statement. He finally pointed his staff in the direction of the underground river. "You have found water."

"Yes."

Nebo studied Jim a moment more, finally reached into a fold of his robe. There must have been a pocket, because he pulled out what looked like a large, dry biscuit. He tossed it to the young human. Jim grabbed it out of the air, gave it only a brief sniff before taking a bite.

It didn't have much flavor, either good or bad, but he began salivating with hunger as he chewed. After two bites, and two swallows, Jim slowed.

"Do you live in here?" he asked, chewing and swallowing his third bite.

"From time to time," said Nebo, watching Jim eat. He cocked his head to one side, then, warily eyed the human. "Have you seen another... like me?"

"I haven't seen anyone."

Nebo looked about the cavern, this time more studiously. He frowned.

"I seek Hishta," he said. He sounded faintly anxious.

"Is that your wife?"

Nebo suddenly rolled his head back and laughed. Jim's question apparently struck Nebo as very funny.

"No, human, no! Hishta *sister*!"

Jim recovered from Nebo's outburst and swallowed the last of the large biscuit. He felt awkward talking at such a distance, as they were still four steps apart, but as yet he wasn't too keen on getting any closer to the little alien. He finally took one small step.

"Is she lost?" he asked.

Nebo's expression grew very serious. He leaned forward on his staff. "Perhaps. Perhaps not. In here, it can be very bad. Outside, it can be worse. There are many dangers. In here. Out there."

Nebo pulled back, brought his staff to his side. He tilted his head back, to one side, to the other. Jim couldn't tell if the alien was listening, looking or smelling. Maybe all three...

"Would you like me to help you find her?" Jim asked. "Your sister?"

Nebo brought his gaze forward, looked curiously at the human.

"Are you not also lost?"

"I don't know," said Jim. He hadn't thought about that. He had crashed on a hostile planet. He had traveled across a desert plain and was wandering in the tunnel maze of a rocky peak. "I mean, I don't really know where I am, but does that mean I'm lost?"

"Interesting."

"I can still help you look."

Nebo suddenly turned about and spoke sharply. "Very well. You can come with me. We can look together."

With that, Nebo started down the next tunnel. He immediately began tapping his staff against the tunnel wall. Jim hurried after him. He didn't think that he would lose Nebo, not with that incessant tapping, but the tunnel was pitch black beyond the circle of light formed by Nebo's lantern.

Jim was much taller than Nebo, and able to see over the little man's head and into the tunnel beyond. For the first time, he was able to see the sandpaper-smooth surface of the tunnel walls and floor, the shimmering of particles within the rock.

They passed a number of side tunnels, some so small that only Nebo would have been able to enter into without bending over. Each time, after only a few moments and a few taps of the staff on stone, Nebo chose to continue down the main tunnel.

"Why do you do that?" Jim finally asked. Nebo continued tapping the wooden staff against the wall of the tunnel.

"Do what?"

"That. Why do you tap your staff against the wall?"

"It lets those whom I do not wish to see know that I am coming."

"Like wild animals? Does that scare them off?"

"No," Nebo stated flatly. "Not wild animals. I do not scare anyone. They do not wish to see me any more than I wish to see them. I give them time to remove themselves from my path."

"I see," said Jim. He wasn't sure that he saw at all.

"Hishta... Hishta will know it is Nebo," said Nebo. "It is easier than calling to her."

Now that, Jim understood. But as for the other, what was out there in the dark that Nebo didn't want to meet up with, if not wild animals?

What dangers might exist in these tunnels?

Nebo stopped suddenly.

Ahead of them, the tunnel forked into two passageways. Nebo was looking cautiously down the left tunnel and listening intently.

"What's wrong?" Jim whispered.

Nebo did not answer. After a few moments, he looked down the right tunnel. There was a faint glow coming from somewhere beyond the bend.

"That is the way out of the peak," said Nebo. "That is the way you should go."

Jim looked to the dull glow emanating from the right tunnel. He then looked into the darkness of the left tunnel. Despite Nebo's ominous tone when he spoke of those whom he did not wish to meet, Jim nonetheless would rather continue with Nebo than step back out onto the hot terrain outside.

He indicated the left tunnel. "Hishta went that way?"

"I am not certain," Nebo stated.

"But you think so."

"Perhaps."

"Then I will go with you," said Jim.

"You should leave the peak."

"Why?"

"There are dangers in here."

Jim indicated the right tunnel. "There are dangers out there."

"That is true," said Nebo. "Very well." He started down the left tunnel, again leaving Jim to hurry after him.

The two traveled in silence but for the sharp clicking of Nebo's staff against the walls of the dark, cool passageway. Time seemed not to exist within the peak, as if the universe had stopped and Jim and Nebo were traveling in the space between one second and the next, and all the rest of the world was waiting for them to reach some unseen point in space and time.

The coolness of the air within the tunnels began to take on humid warmth, growing steadily heavier. Jim felt himself pushing against the thick atmosphere as he went forward, step by step.

And then Nebo's steady tapping of wooden staff against stone wall began to slow.

Nebo stopped.

The air was still. Without the *click, click, click*, the tunnel was oppressively quiet. The only sounds were those of Jim and Nebo's breathing.

And then there came another sound...

Jim wasn't sure at first that he had really heard it, but it grew steadily louder, from barely perceptible to clear and distinct.

It was a gritty, abrasive sound; as of something rubbing coarsely against stone.

"What is that?" Jim whispered.

Nebo said nothing.

"Is that what you were talking about? Is that what you were tapping at, to warn away?"

"Yes."

"Then why isn't it going away?"

"I could not say with certainty, but if I had to guess... perhaps it wishes to speak with us."

Jim felt a sudden chill. He shouldn't feel a chill. The air here was warm.

"What is it?" he asked.

"It is Tunnel Maker."

Chapter Three

The tunnel ahead lost its light as something filled up the space. Nebo held up his lantern and stood immobile, his staff held to one side.

Directly before them appeared a long, snake-like mole creature, short rear legs barely visible at the back of a smooth body, its front legs more like arms, its hands with long, narrow fingers.

Most striking though, was its massive head, which was almost as wide as the tunnel itself, that rested on a slowly twisting neck.

"Wow," Jim whispered.

"Tunnel Maker," Nebo mumbled softly.

Tunnel Maker stopped about six feet in front of Nebo. The air between them was warm and damp. The breath of the creature was hot.

It looked beyond Nebo at Jim with small, dark eyes, and leaned forward as if to get a better look. The thought struck Jim that the creature probably had poor vision. Living down in the dark, it probably didn't use its eyes much, instead relying on its other senses.

It looked decisively at Nebo, sniffed at the air. When it spoke, it was with a smooth voice, and yet the tone was direct. The language was very alien to Jim. The only sound he recognized was when the creature spoke Nebo's name.

Nebo responded in the same language. Without the smoothness of Tunnel Maker's speech, the words came out as little more than grunts and squeaks and gurgling sounds.

Tunnel Maker responded quickly to whatever Nebo said. The words seemed harsher this time. It was not happy.

Nebo spoke then over his shoulder.

"He does not recognize your smell, human. What he does not know, he does not like."

"What's wrong with my smell?"

"What he does not like, he does not trust. He feels threatened by you."

Nebo turned his attention back to Tunnel Maker and spoke again in the creature's language. They appeared to argue back and forth. Jim took a step back, hoping to appear less threatening.

The discussion between Nebo and Tunnel Maker stopped and started several times, and during each silence Nebo would stand unmoving, and Tunnel Maker would slowly ease its massive head forward and back.

And then Nebo sharply spoke half a dozen words and nodded curtly. A moment later Tunnel Maker squirmed and writhed and began to slither backward. Its face faded into the darkness until it was finally completely lost from view.

After a few long moments, it must have started down a side tunnel, because Jim again heard the strange gritty noise coming out of the black, the rasping sound of the creature's body rubbing against the walls of the tunnel.

"Is everything all right?" asked Jim.

"Well enough," said Nebo. He turned sharply and there was a hint of concern in his expression and stance. "We must go."

There was a sudden urgency in the tone, and Jim again began to feel uneasy.

"He and his friends coming back?"

"Of course not," said Nebo, and he started forward at a quick pace. He was no longer tapping his staff.

Jim followed right behind him, easily keeping up with the little man. "He had news of Hishta?"

"We must travel up to the sky."

Nebo's pace was steady, his step sure and focused. He seemed to know exactly where he was going and he obviously wanted to get there quickly. Without the constant *click, click, click* of the staff, the tunnels were strangely empty and silent.

They traveled up, always up, climbing higher and higher within the peak. The yellow sphere of light from Nebo's lantern pushed ahead of them in one tunnel after another, exposing one side tunnel after another. Again and again Nebo would turn suddenly down one of the side tunnels, somehow knowing, or somehow sensing, that this was the correct route.

And time after time, without warning, the glowing sphere of light from Nebo's lantern would suddenly burst out in all directions as the tunnel emptied into some cavern, walls spreading out away from them, ceiling rising up into the dark beyond the reach of the light.

Jim felt his thirst returning, as well as the pang of hunger. It had been hours since he had eaten the biscuit.

He felt a cool breeze brushing against his face. Several more minutes passed, and the breeze grew more steady.

Then Nebo and Jim stepped out under a night sky.

They came out onto a ledge very near the top of the peak. It looked out over the vast alien plain. The shelf was some twelve feet deep and twenty feet wide, large enough that Jim didn't feel uncomfortable.

Nebo walked to the very edge and stared out across the vast expanse. Moving up beside him, Jim could see what Nebo was looking at.

Far in the distance, the plain was aglow with a cluster of campfires.

"What is that?" asked Jim.

"That is the All."

"All?"

"That is what they call themselves, so that is what we call them."

Jim nodded uncertainly. "You knew they were there?"

"No."

"Oh," Jim mumbled. "You came up here to look for them?"

"That is correct."

"Hishta is with them?"

Nebo let out a low, fluttering breath. He had a very worried look on his face. "The All are a peculiar race. They think very logically, but they use that logic to twist events and situations to suit their needs."

"Sounds pretty normal to me."

Nebo's worried expression darkened. "Hishta and I have crossed paths with them many times. They have no doubt used these confrontations to justify taking her."

"What do they want with her?"

Nebo turned away from the edge and walked to the far side of the ledge. He stepped around a recently used campsite. Stones encircled a small fire pit. Near the pit were two piles of dried vegetation that looked like they had been used as bedding. To one side was a bundle of wood bound together with twine.

It had to have taken some effort to bring firewood all the way up here.

Nebo gathered some of the smaller kindling and began to prepare a fire.

"They will sell her," he stated.

"They can do that?"

"There are circumstances in which being sold into bondage serves as payment for crimes or debts."

"But that's not right."

"It is not."

Nebo rose from the small fire that he had started and settled onto one of the beds. He pulled a ball of cloth from one of his many hidden pockets and carefully unfolded it, revealing a round of bread. He tore a piece from the round and handed it to Jim.

"Eat. Then sleep," he said.

When Jim woke in the morning, the air was very cold, the sky was slate gray before the rise of the first sun. Nebo was stirring the fire to life.

Jim slid nearer the rising flames, looked out across the plain in the direction of the camp of the All. He could just make out the silhouette of a very large, boxlike vehicle.

"What is that thing?"

Nebo handed Jim a thick wedge of cheese and a biscuit. He spoke without looking up. "An All transport." He stood then, picked up his staff and pointed it toward a different horizon, where Jim could make out a smear of a shadow. "Beyond the forest is the City of Shannyn. It is many days travel from here. That is where you must go."

"I'm going with you."

"You must not."

"Why not?"

"Shannyn is the largest city on ShadowWorld. The space port is there. Your rescue is there."

"What about you? What about Hishta?"

Nebo indicated the All encampment.

"My path lay there."

"Then so does mine," Jim said flatly.

Nebo smiled sadly. "Young human, the thought warms me; but you would risk your only hope for rescue in a cause that is almost certain to fail. For this, you should not concern yourself."

"I want to help," said Jim. "I can go to Shannyn anytime."

"If you come with me, you may indeed see the city, but it would be as a captive."

Jim tore at the biscuit, put a piece into his mouth.

"I'll take my chances."

Nebo stood and handed Jim a water flask. Jim took a big swallow and handed it back. Nebo continued to stare silently at the human until Jim finally had to turn away from the calm gaze. He frowned, finally turned again to face the alien.

"Maybe... maybe I just don't want to be alone," said Jim.

Nebo studied Jim a moment more before giving a knowing nod.

"Come then," he said. "I leave now."

§

With both suns high in the sky, the desert plain grew increasingly hot. This didn't seem to bother Nebo very much, and the small being continued a steady pace across the landscape. Jim said nothing, not wanting to admit that maybe Nebo would have been better off without him.

After several hours march, Nebo handed Jim the water flask without saying a word, and Jim had to drink as they walked.

They didn't stop until midday, when they reached a small cluster of tiny hills covered in small trees and shrubs. Nebo led Jim into a gulley running between several of the hills. There they sat in the relative cool of the shadow of one of the trees and in the protection of the surrounding shrubs and rise of the hillsides.

Jim saw then that the morning's journey had indeed taken its toll on Nebo. He was nearly spent. He had pushed them both in order to get them here before the day grew truly hot.

"There," said Nebo. He pointed to a spot in the ground, a depression set into the small hillock beside Jim. Jim held out his hand and set his palm on the cool earth.

"Here?"

"Dig."

Jim gave him a curious side-glance but did as he was asked. He scooped out handfuls of earth with one hand at first, before shifting position and using both hands.

He uncovered a buried cache of supplies, pulling out a cloth bundle. Unfolding it, he found several small metal boxes and two ceramic water flasks.

"Food and water," said Nebo. He moved over to Jim and took one of the boxes. Inside were two rounds of cheese wrapped in cloth. He handed one to Jim and began eating the other.

§

They waited until the first sun was low on the horizon before moving out again, away from the protection of the natural shelter. The air was heavy and hot, but slowly began to cool as the larger sun fell nearer the horizon.

They reached the All encampment an hour before the second sun had set. A long shadow stretched out from a low ridge along the perimeter of the camp. Jim and Nebo scrambled within the shadow and crawled on hands and feet up to the top of the ridge.

The camp was spread out across a wide area, several hundred feet from left to right and just as far across. The massive, boxlike transport vehicle was parked along one side. Beside it were two smaller personal vehicles.

There were a number of individual campsites scattered about the encampment. At each, there were water barrels, benches, tables and chairs.

The All were everywhere. They were short, squat, hairy creatures. Their thin, bony arms seemed to come directly out of the sides of their bodies. They moved quickly from place to place. When they stopped to talk with one another, they would rise up and down in sudden jerks. Jim thought maybe the movement was part of their language.

He saw Hishta sitting alone at one of the campsites on the far side of the encampment. She looked as though she could have been Nebo's twin. Perhaps she was.

"There she is," he said to Nebo.

Nebo nodded curtly. He had seen her. He pointed to a campsite near the transport vehicle. A human man and a human woman sat glumly beside the camp fire.

"Do you know them?" he asked.

"No. Yes," said Jim. "Well, sort of. They were in the shuttle with me when we crashed. I didn't know what happened to them. How'd they get here?"

"There are only two possibilities that come to mind. They were taken captive at the crash site, or they were taken captive once they left the crash site."

Oh, that's real helpful, thought Jim, but he said nothing. Instead he studied the perimeter of the large encampment. There was a low ridge in front of the All transport that might offer Jim cover enough to get him close to the human couple. But there would still be a good thirty feet from the top of the rise down to the campsite.

Reaching Hishta looked even more daunting. They would have to walk in a wide circle and come back through a small grove of scrubby trees, and from there to Hishta was at least fifty feet.

Neither looked possible without detection.

Nebo had been conducting a similar examination of the camp.

"I would say difficult, but not completely impossible," he said. "You should work your way around behind their transport vehicle, come in behind the ridge. While you go to your human companions, I will go around and approach Hishta from the grove."

"That's about how I figure it," said Jim. "Nebo... what do we do once we reach them?"

Nebo's face scrunched up as he brought his lips together into a tight, uncomfortable expression.

"Ah," he grunted.

When he didn't say anything further, Jim prompted him. "Nebo?"

"They are not bound," Nebo said at last.

The two humans were sitting on their own, hands and feet free. Looking to Hishta, she was also unbound and on her own.

Jim thought this was a good thing.

Nebo did not. "This concerns me," he stated.

"But why?"

"Hishta and your human comrades do not consider escape to be possible. Neither are the All much concerned that the captives will attempt an escape."

Jim scooted around and into a position where he could again study the camp.

There were a lot of All. At any one moment, the two humans and Hishta were always within sight of dozens of them. And, while the captives were indeed not too far from the perimeter of the camp, there was still some distance to any cover.

Jim looked beyond the camp, at the desert plain that surrounded them.

"I see," he said. What would do once they did make it away from the camp. They were a long way from anywhere, and would likely be picked up again at the leisure of the All. "So, what do we do now?"

"You are free to do as you wish, Jim," said Nebo. "I go to Hishta."

Jim crawled the last few feet up and peered over the top of the low ridge. The man and woman were sitting beside the campfire thirty feet away, at the foot of the hill. The man was leaning close to the woman, speaking low, always with an eye to the All that were moving about the encampment.

Eight feet from the couple was a heavy bench on which sat two water barrels. As Jim watched, an All came up the barrels, filled a metal cup at a spigot and drank. It returned the cup to its hook, looked disinterestedly at the human couple, and went on about its business.

Jim was pretty sure that he could reach the water barrels, and once behind the barrels, he would be out of sight of most of the camp. From there, he could get the attention of the humans.

And get a drink of water...

That thought was enough to urge Jim on. He lifted himself up and slid over the top of the ridge, slid down the other side and pushed himself forward, before finally rising up onto his knees and scrambling downhill towards the bench and the water barrels.

Using the shadow of the barrels for cover, Jim scooted around and looked out across the camp for any indication that he had been seen.

Satisfied that for the moment he was safe, or at least relatively so, he pulled back and leaned against one of the barrels.

It felt cool to the touch. He could smell the water inside the wooden cask.

The metal cup was hanging on a hook beside the spout, on the other side of the barrel... the side facing the camp.

Jim was really thirsty.

He slid back around, reached carefully over and lifted the cup off the hook. He eased back around out of sight.

A moment passed and there was no sudden onrush of aliens.

Emboldened, Jim moved forward again and held the cup beneath the spout. He had to move his body a bit further in order to open the spigot.

He turned the spigot just a little. The sound of water coming out was louder than he expected. He stiffened at the noise, hurriedly turned the handle back and moved quickly back behind the barrel.

Afraid to move, he stared down into the cup, again listening for an onslaught of All rushing to capture him.

The metal cup was half full. The smell of fresh water rose up and tingled his nose.

When, after several moments, no alarm sounded, Jim brought the cup slowly up to his lips and sipped delicately at the water. He drank slowly, felt the liquid work its way down, soothing his throat and settling coolly into his stomach.

Jim glanced again in the direction of the two humans. He was startled to see the man looking at him, an expression of surprise, and something else, on his face.

The man turned quickly away, looked back out to the camp. He appeared determined to keep his eyes away from the water barrels, away from the boy hiding in their shadow.

The woman looked curiously at her companion. She saw that he was upset. The man said something under his breath.

The woman glanced only once in Jim's direction, then she too looked to the center of the encampment.

The man shook his head slowly from side to side, a signal to Jim.

He wants me to leave...

Jim didn't want to leave without them. He wanted to help them. He really wanted to help them.

As importantly, and he knew this in his heart, now that he knew there were others who had survived the crash, he wanted to be with them.

What am I going to do?

Jim looked to either side, then back up the hillside toward the ridge.

With or without them, it was going to be a lot more difficult getting out than it was getting in.

He felt a sudden stabbing pain in his neck.

I've been stung!

He slapped at his neck. There was something metallic sticking out. He pulled it out and looked at it, only half comprehending. A dart?

I've been shot!

He managed to stand, though there was a numbness spreading throughout his body. He managed to shift to one side, looked to the man and the woman.

There were standing too, looking in his direction. The woman held onto the man's arm with both hands, looking at Jim with sympathy. The man's expression hardened with a stiff resignation.

Jim felt thin, bony, alien fingers grasping his arms. He began to fall forward, was pulled back as hands lifted him up. He knew he should be hearing sounds, but there was nothing.

Jim rolled over onto his back. His head felt thick, as if he had been asleep for days.

Asleep...

He *had* been asleep. For how long, he didn't know. He stared up at the ceiling above him. It was metal.

He could feel a rumbling beneath him. There was a sense of movement.

He sat up then and his head spun dizzily. It took a moment for the world to come back into focus.

The room that he was in was moving. He was inside a vehicle.

The transport vehicle?

Jim was certain. He was in the big, boxy transport vehicle.

The rumbling that he felt he could also hear. It was a grumbling background noise that seemed to come from everywhere and from nowhere.

He looked about the room. It was small, perhaps six feet by eight. The only furniture was the cot that he was sitting on. There were no windows, and only one short, narrow door.

Jim stood. As he reached for the handle on the door, it turned suddenly and Jim stepped quickly back. The door opened and two All stood in the opening, one behind the other.

One chittered sharply and rose quickly up and down on its short, thin legs; once, twice.

It stood silent then, seemingly waiting for a response from Jim.

Jim had no idea what the creature wanted.

The second All chittered to the first. Both stepped back into the hallway beyond the door, stopped and waited.

Jim cautiously approached the door and stepped through. As he did, the two aliens turned about and started down the narrow hallway ahead of him.

Small portholes were set into the right wall every three paces at about the height of the All line of sight. Leaning down at one of these, Jim saw that they were traveling across the desert plain. He was at least forty feet above the ground, which meant that there were one or two floors below the one that they were on.

Doors were set into the left wall. All were closed.

This part of the massive transport was quiet but for the deep rumbling of the engines and the reverberations of the great wheels rolling beneath them.

They passed through an open hatch that separated one section of the vehicle from another. A few steps further and Jim noticed an odor in the air.

He could smell food. Real food... Bread and cheese was all well and good, but the thought of real food made him dizzy all over again. The smell emanating from somewhere up ahead made him salivate.

The doors along this section were set farther apart. The All stopped at the third door; they stood on either side and turned about. The nearer All chittered once, rose up and down once, and waited.

Jim stepped up to the closed door, glanced at the All then again at the door.

There might be food on the other side.

He pushed down on the handle and pushed the door open.

He stepped into a large room—a mess hall. There were half a dozen long tables, all but one of them occupied by All. They turned as he entered and looked at him with open curiosity.

There was a counter on the other side of the room where one of the All was filling a bowl with thick soup that it spooned from a pot. Jim was too hungry to be overly cautious, so he walked bravely through the tables and the All and picked up a bowl for himself. He quickly filled it, took a spoon and sat at the only unoccupied table.

He didn't recognize what was in the soup, and didn't recognize the smell, but it didn't taste bad.

After several uncomfortable moments, most of the All turned away from the human and began talking again amongst themselves. None of it made any sense to Jim. The language was made up of sounds that were impossible for humans to make, and included body gestures; gestures that were apparently different when one was sitting than when one was standing.

Encouraged by his earlier success, Jim rose confidently and served himself a second helping of soup. As he spooned the soup into the bowl, he noticed the large container sitting at the far end of the counter. It was filled with a sweet-smelling liquid. Beside the container was a tray of ceramic cups. Jim poured himself some drink to wash down the thick soup.

The All in the room seemed to grow uneasy at the young human's abrupt boldness. They were very clearly unsettled by something in the manner of the alien in their midst.

Jim finished his meal under wary eyes. As he put down the spoon and slid back from the table, ready to stand up and leave, the room again became very quiet. All eyes watched his every move. Very slowly then, Jim rose the rest of the way to his feet. He felt a rising tension in the room. He took several short, easy, non-threatening steps toward the door.

One of the aliens rose up onto its toes, then down, quickly. Up, down, up, down. Not quite a hop, but close.

It began chittering away sharply in its alien tongue.

Jim stopped. He didn't yet sense actual danger, but felt that at any moment he might do something inappropriate, cross some unseen line, and that these creatures might then turn on him.

The longer he stood there, the more unnerved the aliens became. The chittering grew louder and their movements quickened. Several of them moved nearer, their up and down movements propelling them forward.

Jim found himself being escorted to the door. As he reached it, backed into it, the door opened and he found himself standing out in the hall, the two All guards waiting on either side of him, just as he had left them.

They, at least, seemed calm enough. They turned without comment, one leading the way and the other following behind Jim. They passed several more doors and stepped through another hatchway before the lead All stopped. Jim almost bumped into him.

The All seemed to be waiting for something to happen. A moment later, the floor plate beneath them shimmied and began rising; the ceiling overhead slid aside just in time for them to pass through. The timing was designed for lift passengers the height of the All, so for Jim it had been a close call.

The room above was large and dark, but alive with activity. Aliens were squatting in strange chairs designed for their physique. They were studying light patterns displayed on consoles in front of them, occasionally making adjustments, turning knobs and sliding small levers. As Jim watched, one of the All dimmed one of the lights before him, called to another who then turned on one of his. There was a deep rumble somewhere within the vehicle and Jim felt a change in motion.

Jim's escort led him across the room and down another long, narrow hall. The sounds of the control room quickly faded behind him.

The lead escort pushed aside a door and stepped quickly to one side. The rear guard pushed Jim through and he heard the door close behind him with a solid thump.

Jim stood before the leader of the All.

Leader studied the human from across the sparsely furnished room. There was a small table set against one wall on which were several monitors.

There was another of the oddly designed chairs in the middle of the room beside a low table.

Leader began making strange movements with its lips. It didn't make any sounds at first, just moved its lips, as if trying to sort out how it was going to speak.

"Please – forgive – my – talk," said Leader at last. It was a very peculiar sound, but completely recognizable. It was a squeaky sound, almost machine-like.

Leader must have worked long and hard over the years to be able to speak Earth.

It wasn't so much the memorizing of the words that would have been difficult. What was remarkable was for an alien with the All design of mouth and throat to be able to speak the language at all.

"You speak my language very well," said Jim.

"I – speak – fourteen – galactic – languages."

"I speak only Earth language."

"I – assumed." Leader rose quickly up and down, up and down, then stopped. Jim waited until he was sure that it was finished with whatever it was doing.

"What do you want of me?" asked Jim.

Leader showed an expression that Jim found impossible to read. Curiosity? Bewilderment? Amusement? It said nothing.

"Please," Jim said politely. "Am I a prisoner? I would like help to get home."

Several changes of emotion washed over Leader's face.

"Human," it stated. "Minds – of – you – of – All – not – same. Think – *different*."

"I can see that."

"You – here – because – you – die – if – you – not – here." Leader chittered once and rose up and down on its toes. "Out – there – alone – you – die."

"Maybe."

"You – here – alive."

"Yes. For now."

"You... – *stay*."

The room grew ominously silent. Leader made small movements with its face and fingers. Jim grew increasingly uncomfortable.

Watching Leader, watching its facial movements, its gestures, Jim began to think that it was reacting to the series of emotions that Jim was feeling. Just as the aliens in the mess hall had seemingly responded to Jim's increasing self-assuredness.

"How long? How long do I have to stay?"

Leader moved its head back slowly, pausing in what looked to be a thinking pose. After several long moments, it made what it assumed to be the appropriate response to the question.

"Human – be – fed – and – cared – for," it stated. "No more – allowed – freedom – of – ship."

Freedom of ship? Had he had the freedom of the transport? Maybe his door had been unlocked, but he hadn't been awake to take advantage of it.

"All – uncomfortable – with – human. – Human – feelings... – loud." Leader's expression changed to something very much like a grimace. " – Loud."

"What are you going to do with me? How long do I have to be here?"

Leader ignored the question, continued with its own line of thought.

"Human – thinking – different – than – All. Human – actions – based – on – emotions. Human – emotions – *feel* – too – strong, – too – disturbing – to All." Leader made a sound that was a combination of a chitter and a grunt. "Bad – for – All."

With that, the door behind Jim opened and he was led away.

Chapter Four

Jim stared dully up at the ceiling. The vibration of the vehicle's wheels rumbling over the plain lulled him into an odd sense of tranquility. Isolated in his small, stark cell, with only the grumbling sound of the engines coming from some distant room and the faint light glowing yellow from a small panel on the wall, Jim felt strangely calm.

Since being returned to his cell, his captors brought his meals to him. At least two days had passed, and the vehicle had only stopped once. He had hoped they were setting up camp and that he would be let out and allowed to visit with the other captives, but after only a few minutes, the vehicle was again on the move.

He wondered about Nebo. Had he been captured as well? Had he freed Hishta? He liked to think that Nebo and his sister were safely back at the peak.

The door opened and an All placed a plate and cup on the floor of his cell, quickly closed the door again and was gone.

Jim swung his legs around and sat up, bent over and picked up his lunch. Or was it dinner? He wasn't sure.

With no window in his cell, he was unable to use the rising and setting of the suns as a guide. He couldn't be sure that his captors were bringing his meals on a set schedule, so he couldn't rely on the number of meals. Every meal consisted of the same soup that he had eaten in the mess hall, so he couldn't even use the content of the meals.

He judged the passing of time by his sleep periods. He couldn't completely rely on this, as he couldn't be sure his captors weren't watching and then bringing him his "breakfast" each time he woke up.

What if he was only sleeping a few hours at a time?

He had taken only two bites of this latest meal when he heard the latch on the door. He glanced up curiously as the door swung open.

This hadn't happened before. They always gave him more than enough time to finish the soup.

It shouldn't be opening now...

A human stood in the doorway; it was the man. He had to lean down quite a bit to put his head into the room.

"Come on, boy," he whispered sharply.

Jim set the plate aside, quickly stood and followed him out the door even as the man hurried down the narrow hall. Just a few doors down, he turned and left the hall.

The cell was larger than Jim's, but not much. There was a three-legged stool, a small table, and two cots.

The woman was sitting patiently on one of the cots. When the man closed the door behind Jim, she moved quickly, standing and pulling the cot away from the wall. Jim could see that they had managed to take up some of the metal floor, folding it back enough that a body could just get through.

The woman knelt beside the hole and began using a short length of pipe to pry at the lower section of floor, what would be the ceiling of the room below.

"Well?" the man asked. He took the two steps and knelt beside her.

"Almost," said the woman. There was a loud pop as a metal rivet pulled free. The man and woman froze, looked at each other anxiously. They listened for any indication that they had been heard. When no one rushed into the room to drag them away, the man reached into the hole with his bare hands. The woman climbed to her feet and watched him work to enlarge the opening.

The man glanced once at Jim as he worked.

"Twice now we thought you were dead, boy."

"Jim."

"Right. Jim. I'm Robert. That's Ann."

"Hey," said Jim.

"We didn't think you had survived the crash."

"I thought I was alone," said Jim.

"I'm sorry," said Ann. "We did look for you."

Robert grimaced as he pulled up the plating. "We were picked up, rescued we thought—"

"Thought wrong," Ann said sharply.

"—not long after we crashed." Robert nodded brusquely. "I think I've got it, Ann."

Ann knelt beside Robert and the two of them gave the metal plating another pull. It came more freely now and they rolled it back and out of the way.

Robert gave out a loud sigh and looked over at Jim. "There are a lot of ways off this thing, Jim, but this is the only way that we'll make it away alive."

"We're escaping?"

"We certainly are," said Ann.

"That's the plan, anyway," said Robert.

Ann grabbed a cloth bag from the cot, handed it to Robert as she climbed down into the opening. Shifting from side to side in between metal joists, she gave Robert a final nod and dropped out of sight.

Robert laid face down on the floor and slid his head and shoulders into the hole. He dropped the bag down to her. A moment later he lifted himself up onto his elbows.

"Okay, Jim. You're next."

Jim took one step closer to the opening, but remained standing. "What's down there?"

"Our way out," said Robert. "Hurry, now."

Jim moved forward and dropped to his knees before the opening. Robert had him swing his legs around and took him by the arms. When Jim slid in, Robert held his hands and lowered him down.

Ann was waiting below. She took hold of him at the hips and eased him down to the floor of the room.

A ground car was parked in the middle of the room, with not much room to spare. Jim had been lowered down into one corner of the small garage. Along the right wall was a narrow door that Jim guessed led to the main passageway on this floor. Opposite, directly in front of the ground car, was a much larger door.

The sound of the engines of the great transport vehicle was much louder here. The engine room had to be nearby.

Ann went to a set of levers on another wall and studied them. As she did, Robert dropped into the room, went immediately to the vehicle and climbed in behind the wheel.

The car looked much like any other that Jim had been in. It had a front seat, a back seat, four wheels, a steering wheel, and a windshield. But the seats were smaller, sat low to the floor, and were shaped peculiarly, as had been the chairs that Jim had seen. The steering wheel was set an odd angle, as was the dash, which had a confusing array of knobs and indicators.

He was surprised that in this environment of two suns and the heat, that it had no roof. But then, he supposed that it wasn't meant for long distance travel. After all, that was what the much larger transport vehicle was for.

"Ah!" Robert gave a satisfying but muted cheer. A moment later the car engine started.

Ann took hold of one of the levers and gave a pull. The outside wall directly in front of the vehicle began to lower, exposing the world outside. As it lowered, the door formed a ramp down to the ground below.

Robert called to Jim. "In you come!"

Jim climbed into the back seat as Ann hurried around the front of the car and climbed into the front seat beside Robert.

Robert put the vehicle into gear and started it forward. As it passed through the opening, Jim could see only sky and plain, both rushing by from left to right.

The nose of the vehicle dropped down as it started down the ramp. Robert tried to steer the car into the direction that the larger vehicle was traveling, but it wasn't nearly enough. When the front wheels rolled off onto the hard surface of the plain, the back end of the vehicle swung violently around. The car almost rolled over before the back wheels came down hard. It fishtailed back and forth several times before Robert got it under control.

As the large transport vehicle went one direction, Robert turned the car around and took them in the opposite direction. He began working with several buttons set into the dash beside the steering wheel, and after several moments Jim was pressed against the back of the seat as the vehicle suddenly picked up speed.

Seen against the vastness of the desert plain, the speeding vehicle was small and insignificant. It was the only feature in the great expanse of an oppressive alien landscape, above which hovered two unforgiving suns.

To Jim, sitting alone in the back seat, none of that mattered. His head resting on the seatback, he had a relaxed, contented look on his face.

Up in front, Robert offered his wife a supportive smile. They allowed themselves a moment to take in their freedom.

After several hours, the terrain began to change. They had been traveling on the hard, flat surface of the open plain faster than Jim had ever traveled before while still on the ground. But by the time the first sun had set, they began to see small trees and brush. The hardpan beneath the wheels began to soften, becoming more of a soil in which plants could grow. Robert finally had to slow the vehicle in order not to hit something.

Before the second sun went down, they stopped and made camp. Brush formed an enclosing circle around the perimeter, and a tall tree grew nearby that offered a bit of shade to the clearing during the day and allowed the ground to cool in the afternoon. This left the site fairly comfortable in the evening.

Jim remembered how cold it got out on the plain at night, so he was more than happy to help gather firewood from the surrounding vegetation as Ann set about getting a fire going.

"What had you on that cruiser all on your own, Jim?" Robert asked as they collected wood and brush for Ann's campfire. "If it's not too personal."

"I was on my way to Port Kimara," said Jim. "My father got a new job. My parents let me finish school while they went on ahead."

"Kimara?" Robert looked a bit surprised. "Frontier world. Long way from Earth."

"Suppose."

"So you stayed back on Earth to finish up your school year..."

"Stayed with my uncle. It was only a few months," Jim frowned. "Supposed to be..."

"Don't you worry," said Robert. The two of them each had a full armload of twigs and branches.

Ann called out from the struggling fire that she could just barely keep going with what little kindling she had at hand. "You want to bring some of that over here?"

Robert gave Jim a smile and a wink.

"We'll get you on your way again soon enough, Jim. Your parents will hardly have time to start worrying about you.

The night was still and quiet beyond the light of the fire. Robert sat beside it, looking into it. Ann leaned against the parked vehicle, watched the stars overhead as they slowly moved across the sky, clinging to their alien pattern.

Robert continued to tell Jim about the All. "Their minds aren't any better or any worse than ours," he said. "Just different. Alone, in the desert, without them, you would probably die. Therefore, you would choose to stay with them. Logical. For them. But we're not them. We are illogical humans.

"The only reason they locked us up at all and didn't allow us to move about their transport was because our ways made them uncomfortable. We are just too different."

"They never thought we would try to escape?"

"I don't think it would ever have occurred to them." Robert grew thoughtful then. "I don't want you to think badly of them because they think differently than we do, or because they don't happen to be human. Don't ever judge another species along those lines."

Ann spoke up, her words stiff. "Look to their actions."

"Exactly," said Robert. "The actions of the individual."

"Of course," said Jim.

Robert's smile was paternal, that of a parent who is satisfied with his child's answer.

"Good," he said.

"So... what do we do now?"

Robert visibly shifted his thought processes. We head for Shannyn, the main space port on ShadowWorld. It's just a few days' drive from here."

"It is a city of many faces," said Ann, "from all over the galaxy." In spite of the words, she didn't sound as though she was looking forward to going there.

Robert ignored the veiled anxiety. "We should be able to find a way off world."

"What about the All?" asked Jim.

"We may cross paths with some of them. They're desert dwellers, but they do go into the city to trade and barter supplies."

"But won't they try to capture us again?"

"No," said Robert.

"Not once we're in the city," agreed Ann.

"Even if we were to run across the same All, one we're safely out of the desert, their reason to hold us no longer exists."

"Not that we'll be safe," said Ann darkly.

"No worries, Ann," said Robert, comfortingly. "It's no worse than any other port in the frontier."

"That's no comfort."

"We'll be safe enough till we get off Planet."

Before settling in to sleep, they ate half of a round of bread that Robert and Ann had managed to horde away, washed it down with most of the small amount of water they had.

At the rising of the first sun the next morning, they ate the rest of the food. Ann was even more quiet than usual, spent much of the early morning by herself, with her own thoughts. As they prepared to break camp, she wandered over near the vehicle, began to give it the once-over to make sure it was ready for the harsh travel it was about to make.

Robert looked once in her direction, then squatted before the small fire pit. He used a stick to stir dirt into the dying coals. He spoke calmly to Jim as he worked.

"I saw that *Hishta* a couple of times, whenever we were allowed outside. Never talked to her, though. The other one... *Nebo?*" Robert shook his head. "Couldn't say. When they took you, they hauled Ann and me in with you."

Then he could still be free," said Jim. "Maybe he freed Hishta."

Robert stood and tossed the stick into the ashes. He rubbed his hands clean. "Possible, I suppose. You were a bit of a distraction."

Ann looked ready to be off, so Robert and Jim started toward the vehicle.

"The All are one of the few native races to this world," said Robert. "But your friends are another.

They are the Chackee. They know this land. They are at home out here. They are survivors."

Ann climbed in the driver's seat of the vehicle as they reached it. She had overheard the end of the conversation.

"That's why you don't see Chackee in Shannyn. It is an alien world to them." She indicated their surroundings. "As alien as this is to us."

Robert spoke encouragingly, then. "I wouldn't put it past this Nebo. He sounds like a sharp character."

They stopped only once during the day, when they came upon a small creek. It was the first open water that Jim had seen on this world.

The terrain continued to change. The longer they traveled, the more vegetation they saw, and the slower they drove in order to avoid hitting something.

Just after the setting of the second sun, they saw a glow on the horizon.

"The lights of the city," said Robert. "Shannyn."

They traveled for another twenty minutes before they stopped for the night.

They entered the city of Shannyn at midday the following day, Ann again behind the wheel. Large, bright buildings, narrow streets filled with thousands of people from a hundred different worlds.

Some had massive heads and flat, smooth faces, with eyes barely visible behind clear skin. Others had bodies that resembled stick-figures. There were aliens that reminded Jim of tall, thin elves, others that looked like wicked witches from fairytale storybooks.

There were also a handful of All.

As they drove slowly through the crowds, there were very few vehicles other than their own. This drew curious looks from some, but most of those on the street ignored them. This, in spite of the fact that they had yet to see anyone else from Earth or its colonies.

"Stop the car," said Robert, calmly.

Ann pulled off to the side of the road and Robert climbed out. Jim and Ann watched him work his way through the crowd and approach a group of tall, thin beings with pale blue skin, small heads, and long, white hair.

"Chantoo," Ann told Jim. "Honorable people. And fortunately for us, Robert speaks their language."

Jim nodded and relaxed. Maybe this whole thing was almost over.

But when Robert returned, he didn't look all that pleased.

"There's nothing leaving the planet," he said. "All ships are grounded because of the pirate attacks."

"What do we do?" asked Ann.

Robert thought a moment, then straightened and tapped the vehicle with the palm of his hand.

"I don't know how long we're going to be stuck here, but while we're here, we're going to need money. I'll sell the car."

"I don't know, Robert. Do you really think—"

"What's the alternative, Ann?"

"I don't like it." Ann looked and sounded very uncomfortable with the idea.

Meanwhile, Jim quietly took in their conversation, curious as to why Ann would be so concerned.

Robert indicated a square, simple building at the far end of the street.

"You two check into the hotel."

Ann glanced over at the three-storey building. "But—"

"No worries. I'll join you soon."

Ann clearly didn't like the idea of separating, but finally climbed out of the car so that Robert could climb in. "You be careful."

"I promise," said Robert with a smile. He waited for Jim to climb out and then started the car. "I'll be back before you know it."

"You better."

They watched Robert drive away, then crossed the street and went into the hotel.

Inside, they walked across a quiet, cool lobby and up to the check-in counter. The hotel clerk behind the counter was a bulky alien with a large head and a permanent frown.

"We'd like a room, please," said Ann. In spite of the fact that she didn't like the idea of being in Shannyn, interacting with aliens didn't seem to bother her.

The alien responded without changing expression. The words were Earth language, but the way the alien spoke made them sound foreign.

"How long," he said.

"Make it one night... for now."

Once in their room, Ann grew ever more fretful. She went into the bathroom, came out a few moments later with a glass of water. She paced back and forth several times before finally settling into a short, narrow chair.

Jim was glad to be off the street. The crowds outside had begun to make him nervous and he liked the solitude of the hotel room.

From their second floor window, he could see much of the busy, bustling city. There were so many different forms of life, all crowded into the narrow streets of one alien city. He could hear strange voices and very alien languages rising up from the street below.

"I see a human," he said. It was the first that he had seen. This one dressed very oddly, in a style he didn't recognize. It made him look as alien as any other being on the street. "I don't think he's from Earth."

"Very few Earthers come out this far," said Ann.

"Aren't you and Robert from Earth?"

A hint of sadness shadowed her expression. "That was a very long time ago."

Hearing the melancholy in Ann's voice, Jim turned from the window to look at her. She was staring into her water glass. From the look on her face, Jim could see that she didn't want to say any more about it.

"I was on my way to Port Kimara."

"So I understand." Ann took a drink, looked at Jim and tried to smile. "That's a long way from home."

"We're moving there. My parents are there." Jim frowned and turned back to the window. "They'll be worried."

"You'll be with them soon."

Jim nodded tiredly. When he spoke again, it sounded distant. "Another human. I don't think he's from Earth, either."

An hour passed. Then a second went by. By the time the first sun had gone down, Ann was again pacing the room. The city began to glow with the yellow lights that sat atop tall poles lining the major streets. Warm light began to push out from hundreds of small windows.

By the time the second sun had set, the City of Shannyn was alive with night life; bizarre sounds of alien laughter, singing, tavern brawls, angry fighting between the drunken crews of space freighters that had been grounded on ShadowWorld.

Ann put on her light jacket.

"I'm going out to look for him," she said. "You wait here."

"No!" said Jim. "I'm coming with you."

"You have to stay here in case he shows up while I'm gone." Ann was out of the room before he could argue.

Jim stood halfway between the door and window. A sudden, ominous silence hung heavy in the room. He finally turned slowly back to the window, looked out across the alien city. Movement directly below caught Jim's attention, and looking down he saw Ann appear in the street. She moved quickly away from the hotel and disappeared into the night crowd.

He was alone again.

Jim woke with a start.

He hadn't meant to fall asleep, but sometime during the night he had dozed off. Realizing that Robert and Ann had still not returned, he got up from the chair and went to the window.

The first sun was rising. The city rooftops shone with the first rays of daylight.

Jim opened the window and leaned out, putting his elbows on the sill. The morning breeze brushed across his face. He could smell food cooking. He couldn't help but wonder how many different kinds of breakfast were being prepared. His stomach grumbled in anticipation.

Footsteps coming from down the street broke the early morning silence. Backing into the window a little, but still allowing enough that he could see, he watched as two figures walked in his direction.

They were human.

The large, muscular man was talking to the thin man. He spoke softly but firmly, in Earth language.

"With the pirate problem taken care of, I want us gone from this forsaken planet."

"Yes, captain," the thin man nodded. "From what I hear, it was quite a firefight up there."

"The ShadowWorld Protectorate wasn't about to let a handful of cutthroats shut down business. At least, not for long."

"Yes, sir. They do need their taxes."

They were walking very quickly, and were already under Jim's window and starting to move away.

"I want the ship ready to leave just as soon as you can get it done. Get the crew together and check the cargo to see—" The captain's words were cut off as they rounded the corner.

Humans.

Humans speaking Earth language.

And they were leaving ShadowWorld... Maybe they were going to Port Kimara. Maybe Earth. It didn't matter. Jim could get off this planet and to somewhere safe.

What about Robert and Ann?

First, he had to get to the captain. He had to convince the captain to take them with him. Then he would look for Robert and Ann. Maybe he could get the captain to help him find them.

Jim rushed out of the room and stumbled down the stairs. As he passed the front desk, the strange looking alien running the hotel called out to him in what Ann had said was the common tongue on

ShadowWorld. Jim had no idea what he was saying, but he sounded upset.

Jim ran past without stopping and hurried outside. He jumped from the front stoop of the hotel and out into the street. He turned right and ran.

He reached the first intersection and looked down the cross street. He saw the figures of the captain and his first officer far ahead, continuing to walk away from him.

Some shadow of motion made Jim glance in the other direction.

Three large, hairy creatures were pulling a cart down the center of the narrow roadway, a wooden cage riding atop the cart.

In the cage were Robert and Ann, their hands and feet bound with rope.

Jim looked apprehensively back in the direction of the captain. He and his companion turned right and were lost from Jim's view.

Looking back to Robert and Ann, the aliens were just turning the cart down a side street.

It took Jim only a moment to decide. He followed after Robert and Ann.

He reached the next intersection and turned down the street. The aliens and their cart were just ahead. He trailed cautiously after them, careful not to be seen. The street was quiet but for the sound of the cart's wooden wheels rolling over the rough surface of the street.

Jim wasn't sure what he was going to do. For the moment, he watched and waited and followed. He was close enough that he could see Robert and Ann calmly struggling to free themselves of their bonds. Their captors paid little mind to them.

Robert suddenly leapt to his feet, as best the height of the cage would allow, and began jumping up and down, screaming and throwing himself about within the cage. This startled the three hairy aliens. They recoiled in surprise, then turned and looked into the cage in shock and dismay.

Moments later, Ann started in. The prisoners were apparently going completely berserk. The three hairy aliens looked at each other anxiously, bewildered as to what the heck had happened to the humans and what to do about it. They had never before had to deal with such strange aliens.

They whimpered amongst themselves. They squealed softly at the humans. One alien reached in to take hold and soothe the female human. Ann frantically scampered back out of reach.

The alien turned and whimpered again to its two companions, moved over to the door of the cage. At that, the others moved up quickly, intending to stop their comrade from making a mistake.

Finally, after several more whimpers and the continued unsettling behavior of the humans, they came to an agreement.

The first made ready at the door of the cage as the other two moved into position and guardedly stood by. Once all were ready, the alien unlocked the cage and warily reached in, attempted to grab onto either of the crazed human creatures.

Jim, seeing what Robert and Ann were up to, and without taking the time to analyze what he was about to do, ran down the street toward the cart, screaming and jumping and waving his arms.

All three aliens turned in surprise at the bizarre young human coming out of nowhere, rushing insanely down the street, hurtling toward them on this otherwise quiet morning. It ran past them, circled the cart and rushed past again.

Meanwhile, the two humans in their cart continued with their own fits.

One alien reached out to grab hold of Jim and just missed. Frustrated and growing angry, it started after him.

The second alien looked to the cage, then at the third alien, which now had hold of Ann but didn't know what to do with her. It looked again at the first, which was chasing the young human around and around the cart.

It looked again at the two crazed humans within the cart. Its lips began to flutter in frustration. As the young human and the first alien rushed past yet again, it joined in the chase.

In that instant, Robert kicked at the alien that was holding Ann, jumped out of the cage and pulled the alien aside, knocking it to the ground. As the two of them tumbled to the ground, Ann climbed out of the cage.

The first alien chasing Jim hadn't noticed the other humans were out of the cage, so intent as it was on catching the young one on the loose.

The second alien stopped, however, uncertain as to which way to turn. Robert took advantage of this and began running around the cart, jumping on the alien still lying on the ground each time it tried to stand up.

The first alien finally saw what was happening. It stopped suddenly and turned to Robert. Robert crashed into the second, frustrated alien. It fell onto its rump, lips quivering and cheeks puffing.

Ann turned and raced down the street, screaming and jumping, arms flailing in all directions.

Jim quickly followed after her, screaming and jumping and arms waving.

Robert jumped over the fallen alien one final time and hurried after Ann and Jim, also screaming and jumping and arms flailing.

One alien chased after the humans. Back at the cart, one hairy alien rested on its backside, lips fluttering, while the third had crawled beneath the cart to avoid being stepped on.

Jim raced down one street, then another, following Ann, who was turning at each intersection. The only sounds were those of their pounding footsteps echoing ahead of them.

Looking back over his shoulder, Jim saw Robert some distance behind, with the alien right at his heels.

Robert gave a quick wave to Jim and then turned off the street. The alien followed Robert. Jim stopped, looked to Ann, and then back to the path the Robert had taken.

When Ann saw Jim stop, she stopped. She waved frantically for him to follow. After several seconds, he started again.

Ahead, Ann turned down another street. Reaching it, Jim turned.

Ann was nowhere in sight.

Jim paused only a few moments and then started slowly ahead. He looked down each side street that he passed, kept going forward.

He almost ran into the captain.

"Hold on there, son," said the captain. He placed a heavy hand on Jim's shoulder.

Jim felt a sudden, desperate elation. Here was the very man that he had been hoping to find. His first officer stood dutifully behind him, and beside the first officer was an alien. It took Jim a few seconds, but it finally came to him that it was the clerk from the hotel.

"What's your rush, boy?" asked the captain, a broadening smile on his face.

Jim's mind raced. He blurted out the first thing that popped into his head.

"We crashed."

"Excuse me?"

"Pirates... we escaped... we crashed... I was... I was out in the desert."

"I see."

The captain didn't seem at all surprised by this turn of events. He glanced knowingly over his shoulder at the first officer and the hotel clerk. When he turned back to Jim, he stepped up beside him and started them walking forward. They passed between the others, who quietly made way for them.

"Why don't you tell me what happened?"

When the captain stopped, Jim stopped. The first officer and the hotel clerk, patiently keeping pace behind them, stopped two steps back.

The captain looked sympathetically at Jim.

"That's quite a story, Jim," he said.

"Can you help me?"

"Certainly, young sir."

"And my friends?"

"I will if I can." The captain again placed a hand on Jim's shoulder. This time, however, his fingers gripped a bit uncomfortably. He spoke over his shoulder to his first officer.

"Get some help. Find the couple." The tone was different, more firm. It didn't sound right. It didn't fit with the conversation.

It made Jim feel uneasy. "You can get us off the planet?"

"Absolutely." The captain looked again at his first officer. "Jahkard may already have them. Check with him first."

"Yes sir." The assistant nodded, turned and left.

The hotel clerk looked on expectantly. The captain reached into his pocket with his free hand, pulled out a handful of coins and dropped several, one at a time, into the waiting hands of the alien. It too, then, turned and left.

The captain looked down at Jim.

"I may just pull a decent cargo off this depressing planet after all."

"I don't understand."

"I suppose not," said the captain. He began walking, dragging Jim along with him. "You ran out on a debt you owed the hotel, Jim. That was very, very wrong."

"I was going to find you! To help my friends!"

"Friends? Thieves, both of 'em. Stole a vehicle, tried to sell it. That was very wrong, as well. Why do you think they were in that cage? The Benzagi aren't that bright, but they were only trying to do their duty."

"What?"

"Not to worry, lad. All will be made right. I paid your debt." The captain sighed contentedly. "And I shall pay theirs."

"What..." Jim knew that something was terribly wrong, but couldn't quite sort it out.

"By the laws of Shannyn, you are now my property, boy."

"You can't do that!"

"Of course I can. The law is most definitely on my side in this matter."

"Then the law is wrong."

"I won't argue that," the captain sighed again. "However... right or wrong, it can frequently turn a profit."

"You can't buy people!" Jim struggled to get free, but the captain had a very tight grip on him and kept him off balance as he dragged him along.

"Earth won't let you do this! My father won't let you do this!"

"In point of fact, Earth has little to say in matters concerning the Frontier Worlds; even less about the Outworlds beyond." The captain showed Jim another broad grin. "In any case, very few humans come this far out. You will fetch a very good price indeed."

The captain dragged Jim through a stone gateway guarded by two burly humans. Beyond, in the middle of a large landing field, sat the ship. It was big, squat, almost round, and ugly.

To the left was a fenced enclosure, a thousand feet on a side, containing several hundred aliens of a dozen or more species. The captain handed Jim off to two other guards without another word.

As the captain walked toward a small, wooden building, the guards led Jim to the barbed wire gate and pushed him into the holding pen.

Chapter Five

Jim sat with his back against the wire mesh of the fence that enclosed the large holding yard. The ground beneath him was hard and bare. A cool night breeze blew across his face. He watched as the other captives, hundreds of alien beings of all shapes, sizes and colors, struggled for sleep or milled about dejectedly amongst each other and tiny, makeshift shelters, accepting of their fate as slaves.

He had left his spot by the fence only twice during the day, when the food bins, sitting on benches near the water troughs, were filled and the captives drifted mindlessly over to fill their bowls with the tasteless gruel.

Jim stood slowly now as the bins were filled with the evening meal. Gripping his bowl in hand, he glanced at the gathering crowd and decided that it just wasn't worth it. He stuffed his bowl back into his shirt and turned away, wrapped his fingers into the mesh of the fence and looked out beyond the pen.

Twenty yards from the pen stood a dark, wooden building. Through the open door he could see the tall figure of a man wearing a black cloak. Gathered outside the building was a group of aliens of different species.

As Jim watched, several others came and went, some going inside and doing business with the cloaked figure, others speaking briefly to the aliens and then leaving.

This had been going on through most of the day.

Jim heard the sound of footsteps behind him. He turned in time to see a short figure step up beside him and look through the fence.

Hishta?

"You're from Earth?" she asked, speaking Earth. She continued to gaze half-heartedly at the activity beyond the fence.

She certainly looked like Nebo's sister.

"You're Hishta," said Jim.

The alien looked startled. "How can you know that?"

"I was with Nebo," said Jim. "I was at the peak. We tried to rescue you."

Hishta grumbled low. "Not successful, I would say."

"What about Nebo? Was he captured too?"

"No," Hishta sighed. "He is out there, still."

"That's good."

"Yes. But I fear that he may further endanger himself in another attempt to rescue me."

"He cares very much for you."

"He does." Hishta continued to stare beyond the holding pen. "There is nothing that he can do for me. We are lost."

Jim nodded. He felt empty inside. "What's going to happen to us?" he asked.

"We are being sold to one of the Outworlds." Hishta grimaced. "I believe we are to be taken to one of the planets along the Outer Rim. The work is hard, made harder by the... *unpleasant*... climate."

Hishta looked at Jim as if studying him. "Humans survive the longest. You will bring a good price."

"So I understand," Jim stated flatly. "I'm not staying."

Hishta burst out with a loud laugh. It was sharp and shrill and unexpected. "You will just leave?"

"Yes."

Hishta's expression and tone changed suddenly, to one of empathy. "You sound much like Nebo. You no doubt got along well together."

"Well enough," said Jim, a bit defensively. He rested his hands on the fence, gripped the mesh with his fingers. The cloaked man in the building was alone.

Hishta followed Jim's gaze. "That is Jahkard," she said. "Buyer for our owner."

"No one owns me."

Hishta gave a strange, alien shrug. "As you wish." After a few moments, she spoke softly, without looking at Jim. "It looks as though the buying is complete. I would guess that we will depart in the morning."

Jim nodded, his mind running down a dozen different paths. "Then I must leave tonight," he said at last.

"You have yet to tell me how you intend to accomplish this feat."

Jim looked down at the friendly, innocent face. She would not survive long on one of the Outworlds that she had described.

He looked back through the fence. Beyond the small building was a high, stone fence. If this was like other space ports, this field would be surrounded by that enclosing stone barrier.

"What's beyond that wall?" he asked.

"Other landing fields," said Hishta. "Beyond those, the City of Shannyn, of course."

Jim gripped tightly at the fence. Getting over this fence would be easy enough, but reaching the wall, and then finding a way through the gate, unseen, was doubtful; even in the dark.

Getting out of the holding pen unseen... difficult.

And if he could get out of the holding pen, then getting out of the landing field unseen... difficult.

How to get out of the holding pen in such a way that getting out of the landing field was possible?

"Human?" asked Hishta, curious as to Jim's strange lost gaze.

"My name's Jim."

"Jim. You have a way out of our seemingly inescapable predicament?"

Jim had a sudden thought. He wasn't sure where it came from...

"We need to find soft ground."

"In the holding pen?"

"Preferably." Jim tried to hide the sarcasm.

The little alien crinkled her face into a heavy frown, thinking. "I don't know," she said finally.

"Dark soil, not too smooth; out of the way."

"You do not expect to dig your way out of here, do you, Jim?"

"Of course not," said Jim. "Well, not exactly."

"Under the water troughs?" asked Hishta doubtfully.

Jim glanced in the direction of the troughs.

Wet and dark and disturbed from heavy traffic underfoot.

"Maybe."

The troughs were along the side fence. When not in use during meals, the prisoners tended to stay within easy walking distance but not so near as to be bothered by foot traffic. No one would be overly suspicious at seeing fellow captives moving about near the troughs.

Jim stepped away from the fence, began a slow, wandering walk in the direction of the water troughs. Hishta followed beside him.

Around the troughs, as well as beneath, the soil was dark with moisture. Come daylight, the area beneath the troughs would remain in shadow.

Reaching the troughs, Jim walked around to the backside so that he could watch the prisoners. He took his bowl and dipped it into the water, filled it and brought it to his lips. Hishta looked at him curiously, then she took her bowl and did the same.

A prisoner approached. Jim nodded a greeting as the alien filled her bowl with water, warily eyeing Jim.

Jim smiled as the alien walked away.

"What is it you plan to do, Jim?" she asked.

Jim started slowly away from the trough. "Wait for dark," he said.

Most of the prisoners had settled in for the night, though a few continued to wander aimlessly. Kneeling behind one of the troughs, Jim began scraping at the soil beneath with his meal bowl. Hishta watched him uncertainly at first, then knelt beside him and began to help.

The first few inches were easy. After that, it became more difficult. Scraping in the dark, they stopped a number of times, several times to rest, several times to wait for thirsty prisoners to drink and return to their sleeping places.

Jim had Hishta lay in the first of the holes to test for depth three times before he was satisfied.

Using hers as a guide, they dug his beneath the second trough.

Finally completed, no more than an hour before dawn, Jim had Hishta return to her hole and lay in it. He covered her over, spreading the excess soil around the base of the troughs. They had found nothing to use to breathe through, so her nostrils were left just poking up through the surface.

He slid back and examined his work. In the darkness, he could see no sign of Hishta buried beneath the trough. In the daylight, he could not be so sure.

He hoped they would come for the prisoners before dawn.

It was more difficult to bury himself. He covered his legs and body, spreading soil as he gradually laid back. Fully within the hole, he pulled soil to himself, covered his head, then laid one arm along his side and covered it with the other. He covered himself fully, then worked his other arm along his side and wriggled his body about to settle the soil.

He had no way to check for telltale signs. Again he hoped they would come for the prisoners in the dark.

As dawn approached, Jim began to hear footsteps around the troughs as fellow captives came to collect water. He was anxious at first, but as more and more came and went he became increasingly confident that the plan might just succeed. All the activity should eliminate any signs of digging.

Jim's body itched from lack of movement. Tiny grains of wet dirt worked their way into his nostrils.

Movement around the troughs lessened. He then heard what sounded like movement en masse as the hundreds of captives were herded in the opposite direction, away from the troughs.

Finally there was silence.

Jim waited.

The ground began to tremble, the trough above him to vibrate. The very air above him rumbled and roared as the nearby cargo ship lifted up from its pad. For a moment Jim was afraid that he and Hishta might be too near the pad, before mentally calculating that the distance from the pad to the nearby buildings wasn't much greater than to the troughs, and noted that the fence, buildings and troughs had probably survived numerous lift-offs and landings prior to this one.

Jim lay unmoving for several minutes more in the absolute silence that followed the departure of the slave ship. He then raised his head just a little, let the dirt fall away from his face, and turned enough to look out across the holding yard.

It was empty.

He rolled himself out of the hole and out from under the trough. In the distance, beyond the fence, he could see that the door of Jahkard's building was closed.

No one was around.

He crawled forward and laid a hand on the dirt mound that was Hishta.

"I think we're safe," he said quietly. Dirt fell away as Hishta lifted herself up. Jim moved back as she rolled over and out from under the trough.

She looked around them, as Jim had done, then looked at Jim.

"We did it," she said, not fully ready to believe it.

Jim grinned, and his teeth and eyes shimmered from within his dirt-covered face.

"Looks that way," he said.

Hishta managed to hold back her own grin. "You did it."

Jim shrugged. Dirt fell away from his shoulders.

Now Hishta did smile, and brushed dirt from Jim's shirt.

"I think we should get cleaned up," she said.

They cleaned up as best they could at the water troughs; hair, face, hands and arms. Jim took off his shirt and rinsed it out, gave his body a splash, taking off the worst of it.

"Do you know how I can get off this planet?" he asked Hishta as he wrung out his shirt.

Hishta pulled her wet hair back from her face. "The Chantoo," she said. "I am certain they will help."

"Yeah... Ann said they were all right."

"I would agree."

Jim shook out his shirt and pulled it on. "What about you? What will you do?"

"I will find Nebo," she said matter-of-factly. "He will no doubt be nearby."

Hishta led Jim through a maze of narrow lanes lined with sandstone walls. Occasional archways on either side opened out to landing fields of different sizes; some small, some very large. Ships and shuttles sat on pads at safe distances. Small power carts waited inside some of the archways, ready to take passengers and crew out to the spacecraft.

The primary lanes bustled with aliens rushing about. Now that the problem with the pirates had been resolved, the threat taken care of by the ShadowWorld Protectorate, those who had been stranded were now eager to continue on their way.

Freighter crews, losing money each day they were forced to remain planet-side, were eager to deliver their cargo and pick up their next shipments.

They stopped once when Hishta asked directions of a pair of thin, childlike aliens. They nodded kindly and pointed the way.

They turned right onto an even narrower lane...

And came face to face with the tall, dark figure of Jahkard and several of his assistants who were following behind him.

Jahkard stopped in the center of the lane and looked curiously down at the frozen figures of Jim and Hishta. He didn't appear to be angry or concerned. If anything, his expression was one of interest at the unfolding situation.

He smiled pleasantly.

"It is true, then," he said. His voice was smooth and strangely gentle. He exuded calm and confidence. "Just how did you manage this?"

Hishta glanced quickly to Jim without turning her head, then looked sharply up at Jahkard. She held her silence.

Jim shrugged noncommittally.

"Was nothin'," he said.

Jahkard smiled again and nodded.

"I see," he said, pulled absently at one ear. "I'm afraid that my staff have grown overly lax. They didn't realize such a valuable unit in our inventory was missing until well after they were off-planet. The discovery caused quite a stir. Some insisted that you had to be somewhere amongst the cargo and were simply hiding; that you would eventually be found."

Jim and Hishta continue to hold their silence.

Jahkard sighed pleasantly. "And so you have... this should ease the ire of my employer."

"The captain is a monster," said Jim. He couldn't help himself.

"Quite," Jahkard chuckled. "So you'll appreciate my relief in having found you."

At some unseen signal, Jahkard's assistants moved into position, one taking Jim by the arm, the other taking Hishta.

At the same time, a third assistant entered the lane and moved quickly up beside Jahkard. He handed his boss a sheet of paper. Jahkard read silently. When finished, he slowly lowered his hand and studied Jim.

"What's your name, boy?"

"Jim."

Jahkard's expression revealed that, while expected, he didn't particularly like Jim's answer. Still, he tried to maintain his air of calm and confidence.

"Where were you headed, Jim?"

"Port Kimara. To join my family."

Jahkard took a moment to absorb this bit of information, then signaled his assistants to release Jim and Hishta. He managed to restore some of his pleasantness.

"There are some important people attempting to locate you, son. They are quite concerned as to your well being."

"S'pose that would be."

"Word of the attack on the cruise liner reached them rather quickly. Their distress apparently reached ShadowWorld's administrative council as swiftly."

Jahkard bowed his head and looked out from under his brow. He put on his most ingenuous smile.

"I shall relay this latest as to your status and standing to my employer," he said. "Please consider his payment of your debts as his gift to you in your time of trouble."

"I'll do that," said Jim.

Jahkard looked side glance at Hishta. There was a moment of apprehension before Jahkard turned smoothly aside and made way for them to pass.

"The young lady is free to go, as well. That is my gift to you both."

Jim and Hishta moved quickly past the tall, dark figure.

Hishta and Jim turned right and started down a long, much quieter lane. Jim could see three archways spaced several hundred yards apart.

"I believe these are the Chantoo landing fields," said Hishta, a bit uncertainly.

"We still need to find Robert and Ann," said Jim. "I can't leave without them."

"Of course." Hishta did not slow her pace. "First let us speak with the Chantoo. Then we will find your friends."

Looking through the first open archway they came upon, they saw only an empty field and landing pad. There was no ship and no Chantoo.

They continued toward the next archway. The further they traveled from the main thoroughfares, the quieter the world around them became.

After a dozen paces more, Jim began to hear a hollow grinding sound: rubber tires rolling across sandstone... He slowed and looked over his shoulder.

A small electric cart was coming towards them.

"Hishta, wait." Jim reached out and took her by the arm.

He recognized the driver as a Chantoo. The being was tall and thin, with pale blue skin, a small head and long white hair.

Sitting next to the alien was Ann. The figure sitting behind Ann must therefore be Robert though he couldn't see his face.

The driver slowed the cart as it approached Jim and Hishta, stopped directly beside them.

"Well, I'll be..." Robert scooted to one side. "We thought we had lost you yet again. This is getting to be a habit. You might want to work on that, kiddo."

Ann smiled at Hishta. "You must be Hishta."

"That's right," said Hishta.

"I know of someone who will be very pleased to see you."

"Yes?"

"He was certain the two of you were on the ship that lifted off this morning."

"Jim showed great ingenuity in gaining us our freedom," said Hishta. "I owe him my life."

From the back seat, Robert indicated the space that he'd made for Jim.

"Climb in, hero. Not much time."

"Where might I find my brother?" Hishta asked Ann.

"We left him just a few minutes ago," said Ann. "Over near the main port office."

Hishta looked at Jim. "I thank you, Jim."

"All in a night's work," said Jim as he climbed in beside Robert. The Chantoo started the cart forward. Jim called out behind him as they left Hishta behind. "Tell Nebo I said goodbye."

Hishta waved, waited until the cart reached the next archway before she turned about and hurried to find her brother.

The Chantoo driver steered the cart out across a vast landing field toward a small shuttlecraft. Three

Chantoo stood at the ramp beneath the craft. When the cart stopped, one of the waiting aliens began waving for the humans to hurry.

As they stepped up on the ramp, Jim looked at Robert with a growing sense of unease.

Something isn't quite right...

"What's going on?" Jim asked Robert.

Robert nudged Jim along, the two of them following Ann up the ramp.

"Let's just say there are certain folks who would disagree with our departure plans."

"You don't make friends easily, do you Robert?"

"Don't get cute."

They walked quickly into the shuttle. The Chantoo followed in after them even as the ramp started to close. Almost immediately, Jim felt the floor beneath him begin to vibrate. They hurried into the forward cabin and sat down in tall, narrow seats obviously designed for the Chantoo physiology. Jim looked out the small round window and watched the space port fall away below them, the shuttle rushing upward toward the larger spaceship waiting in low orbit.

One of the Chantoo said something to Robert before continuing forward and through another doorway. Robert turned to Ann and Jim.

"We'll be docking with the Chantoo cruiser in a couple of hours. They're scheduled to leave orbit soon after."

Ann visibly relaxed. "Thank goodness."

Jim turned and looked again out through the viewport. The planet below appeared to be covered with shadows. He could see the shimmer that was the City of Shannyn.

Robert could see that the boy was lost in troubled thought.

"What's on your mind, Jim?" he asked.

Jim continued looking out the viewport. It took him a moment to find words, and then the words seemed not to be enough. "It's wrong," he said.

"What's that?"

Jim still didn't seem to know how to answer. Nothing was adequate to his feelings.

"They made me their property," he said flatly.

"Ah," said Robert. "That."

"I got away, but... so many didn't."

Ann looked sadly at Jim. "Out here in the Frontier, there's still an awful lot of bad."

That's not an answer...

There was a very long moment of uncomfortable silence.

"I'm going to change that," Jim finally grumbled.

"Is that so?" Robert smiled gently.

"Yes."

"A very noble sentiment, my boy, and I wish you well. But changes like that tend to be painfully slow in coming."

"Not this time."

Robert was about to respond, but Jim's dark tone and darker expression made him stop. He gave the boy a short nod and turned away. He looked at Ann, as if questioning what they might say to the boy. She didn't look as though she had an answer either.

Jim kept his sharp gaze to the view beyond the window.

A few moments later, a Chantoo entered the passenger compartment with an electronic notepad in hand. He handed it to Robert and left without speaking.

"What is it," asked Ann. She didn't want any surprises at this stage in their rescue.

"Don't know... gimme a sec." Robert silently read the message in the display, then lowered the pad and looked in Jim's direction, the slightest smirk on his face.

"Well?" asked Ann, now with growing impatience.

"Well, Ann," Robert continued to look at Jim. "It appears the Chantoo cruiser that we are soon to board will be making a slight detour en route."

Jim held his silence, held his gaze out the viewport.

"Why?" Ann's impatience had quickly morphed into distress. "What's wrong?"

"Oh, nothing to worry about. Nothing at all. But it seems that we will be making a brief stop at Port Kimara to drop off a passenger."

Ann looked confused at first, then turned Jim.

"Jim... Jim, isn't that where you were going?"

Jim answered without turning from the viewport. "Yes."

When he said nothing further, Ann turned to Robert for answers.

"His father is the new governor of Port Kimara."

"The new—"

Robert looked again directly at Jim. "One of the most powerful positions in the Frontier."

Only now did Jim turn away from the viewport. "My father is not one to flaunt power and position."

"Is that why you were traveling anonymously?" asked Ann.

Jim shrugged in answer.

Robert took a moment to consider this new information. The look of understanding slowly shown on his face.

"Jim, being the son of the governor may open a few doors, particularly after what you've just been through, but make no mistake, the fight you would take on is a very difficult one."

The cabin was silent for a few moments, then Ann spoke softly.

"Robert... Robert, I don't think he has a choice. Do you?"

The cabin was again silent, but for the rumbling of the shuttle's engines. Jim settled back into the alien seat, gazed long through the viewport out at the black of space that surrounded them.

Ann and Robert turned from Jim and looked at each other.

For them, an adventure was ending.

They knew that Jim's was just beginning.

... the end

CPSIA information can be obtained
at www.ICGtesting.com
Printed in the USA
FSHW011951221219
65367FS